Praise for Storyshares

"One of the brightest innovators and game-changers in the education industry."
— Forbes

"Your success in applying research-validated practices to promote literacy serves as a valuable model for other organizations seeking to create evidence-based literacy programs."   — Library of Congress

"We need powerful social and educational innovation, and Storyshares is breaking new ground. The organization addresses critical problems facing our students and teachers. I am excited about the strategies it brings to the collective work of making sure every student has an equal chance in life."
— Teach For America

"It's the perfect idea. There's really nothing like this. I mean, wow, this will be a wonderful experience for young people."   — Andrea Davis Pinkney,
Executive Director, Scholastic

"Reading for meaning opens opportunities for a lifetime of learning. Providing emerging readers with engaging texts that are designed to offer both challeng-es and support for each individual will improve their lives for years to come. Storyshares is a wonderful start."
— David Rose, Co-founder of CAST & UDL

Storyshares presents

Published by Storyshares, LLC
Inspiring reading with a new kind of book.

The characters and events in this book are fictitious. Any similarity
to real persons, living or dead, is entirely coincidental.

Storyshares
Storyshares, LLC
24 N. Bryn Mawr Avenue #340
Bryn Mawr, Pennsylvania 19010-3304
www.storyshares.org

Interest Level: High School
Grade Level Equivalent: 5.8

ISBN 9798885977722
Book design by Saskia Globig

A DIFFERENT KIND OF BLIND

Michael Fergus

Storyshares

CONTENTS

Chapter One —— 9

Chapter Two —— 11

Chapter Three —— 13

Chapter Four —— 17

Chapter Five —— 19

Chapter Six —— 21

Chapter Seven — 23

Chapter Eight —— 27

About the Author — 30

ONE

The sun cooked that apartment complex rooftop.
It had been some time since I had seen my dad's
side of the family, but they and too many random
fourteen-year-olds to count were all up there.

The day before, I had bought new sunglasses.
Chrome with mirrored lenses, by the way. I was
excited to wear them, especially knowing I was
going to such an exclusive setting as a rooftop
party. The family always saw me as "just another
cousin," but I hoped those sunglasses would make
me stand out a bit.

My relatives seeing me as more than just
an audience for them was a funny thought. The

shades were also a much-needed confidence boost going into several socially stifling hours.

They made me feel like somebody when all my relatives made me think I was a nobody.

The stereo thumped a top-forty hit with mumbling lyrics. I stood under the gaudy congratulations banner to the left of the stairwell, bobbing my head slightly. My modest smile hid my inner dread. After a few awkward seconds, I looked down at my phone for a text I knew wasn't there.

"Sleek," I heard someone say to my left, followed by an unconvincing laugh.

The family had this thing where common courtesies like basic greetings were too much to ask for. They'd always try to start a conversation in any other way.

"Mirrored shades?" the voice asked, after I pretended not to hear.

TWO

The smell of exotic, citrusy cologne was an air-
borne spoiler. I looked up from my nonexistent text
and there he was: Cousin Vince.

He was laughably overdressed for an eighth-
grade graduation party with his cream-colored
pants and white loafers without socks. We were
the same age and came from the same upbringing,
but he was dressed like he owned his own night-
club. I did not know where someone would even
buy the outfit he had on, but it was clearly expensive. His father, my dad's brother, was a lawyer.

Vince was the type to think that claiming to be
a social media influencer meant you were one. He

carried himself like he was some fashion expert.

He complimented the mirrored lenses that hid my rolling eyes behind them.

"So, what brand are those, man?" he asked.

"Not sure," I answered.

I wanted to show interest, and not about something trivial, so I asked if he planned to go back to college. His clearly threaded eyebrows crunched together as he rattled off several brand names instead.

I didn't know much about fashion, so every brand he name-dropped sounded like the name of a foreign country to me. Already exhausted from only a couple minutes of social interaction on that rooftop, I could only bring myself to shrug in response.

"Dude, how could you not know?" he asked, clearly irritated.

Although he was looking directly into my mirrored sunglasses, he couldn't see his materialistic, one-track mind staring back at him.

"Let me see them," he said.

I pretended to wave to anyone on the other side of the rooftop, excusing myself in the process.

THREE

I pushed through the mob of troublesome teens, trying to get to the other side of the roof and far away from Vince. It was moments later that I heard a long, piercing shriek. I didn't hear actual words.

I turned to my left, but my aunt Val already had her long, lime-green fingernails dug into my shoulder.

"I didn't know you were coming," she blurted, holding a martini glass in her other hand. "You're never at these sorts of things."

That was true. I did try to avoid "these sorts of things." I found forced socializing to be unnerving.

When I was young, Aunt Val walked around

these gatherings dolled up with lots of makeup. If she had any more on, she could have worked as a clown at birthday parties.

My dad would later tell me that Val went through an "ugly" divorce right around the time I was born. Following the split, she became all about herself. "No man's love could ever equal my self-love," she once drunkenly shouted out at a wedding reception.

Before I could properly greet her, Val was well into her usual spiel about her daughter. Cary was a year older than me. I never saw Cary at "these sorts of things" either, but Val would probably have taken offense if I pointed that out. My mom told me to watch my mouth.

On other occasions where I'd been trapped talking to Val, she'd always talk about Cary as someone I should model myself after. When I asked where Cary was, Val said her daughter was "toughing it out in the heart of NYC."

Cary ran a "jewelry business." Val would make you believe Cary mass-produced products for every store in the city. But she only handmade bracelets every so often and sold them online. I saw them on social media.

I mentioned that my friend from high school, an artist, painted and used a similar business model. However, as soon as I wasn't talking about her daughter, Aunt Val's attention quickly faded.

She began adjusting her platinum blonde bangs while staring right at me. I want to say she pretended to listen, but that would give her too much credit. Things became a bit uncomfortable as she leaned forward awkwardly.

As I tried to keep up the conversation I didn't want to be a part of, I realized something. Val wasn't even looking at me. She was looking at herself.

I stood in front of my aunt as she used my sunglasses as her personal mirror. Val only wanted an audience, and I didn't meet the job requirements once I opened my mouth. She could perfect her looks all she wanted, but she didn't see the glaring narcissism reflecting back.

FOUR

Vince slithered his way over to where I was and jumped into my conversation. I thought he came back still looking for an answer. Instead, he asked Val where Cary was. It was funny, because all he cared to know about me was the brand of sunglasses I was wearing.

Uninterested in a repeat of the sugarcoated story of a young jewelry maker in NYC, I went for my signature stealth sidestep out of the conversation.

Behind the mirrored shades, I could watch the crowd without accidentally making awkward eye contact with anyone. Make no mistake, I had excellent eye contact, despite what my mother said. But not being forced to get into an unwanted conversation just because I'd locked eyes with someone was refreshing.

My name was suddenly called out. I couldn't see her, but I knew my mother's voice anywhere. I sighed and walked over to her. On the bright side, she was one of the lesser evils on that rooftop.

"Well, I'm here, just like you told me to be," I said, with purposeful sass.

"What are those ridiculous things?" my mom instantly asked.

She usually scoffed at my appearance, so this comment was nothing new. She told me she gave me beautiful blue eyes and that I shouldn't hide them.

"The sun is barely even out now," my mom whined as the evening began setting in.

She witnessed my entire lifetime of "antisocial tendencies." So, of course, she accused me of specifically buying these sunglasses to avoid looking my family members in the eye.

"And you better not say anything that I'll have to answer for later," my mom added, looking into the reflections of the sunglasses she apparently hated so much.

I wished she could see that my words or actions had no effect on her reputation in the family.

"You're sure pleasant today," I sarcastically answered.

FIVE

Another cousin, Jill, with her nine-month-old in her arms, cornered the both of us.

"Hello, Jill," I said, giving her baby daughter one of those tiny half-waves.

"Oh my goodness, do you want to hold little Skylar?" she asked with her nasally voice before any kind of greeting.

I was prepared to respectfully say no. But if I hadn't gotten my arms up, Jill would have let go of her child, assuming I was there to grab her.

It wasn't so bad. I stared into the little girl's innocent green eyes and smiled. She smiled back at me, even with one of her hands entirely in her mouth. This was the most pleasant social interaction I'd had all evening.

Skylar saw herself in the reflection of my glasses and giggled some more. Unlike Aunt Val, I couldn't be annoyed by an infant.

Jill and my mom looked at all the fourteen-year-olds, commenting on how old everyone was getting. Skylar's hand, which was now out of her mouth and covered in spit, whacked my sunglasses. Her pure little giggles combatted my inner frustration.

She clapped her hands, so proud of herself. Now, both of her hands were covered in baby slobber. Skylar leaned forward and reached for a lens with each of her tiny hands.

Jill turned around, looking directly into my lenses.

"Oh, remember when we were their age?" she asked.

She turned back toward the party. I tried turning my head away, but Skylar's grip was locked onto my no-longer-brand-new sunglasses.

SIX

"Jill," I said.

I tried to stay calm as I stared at the back of my cousin's head.

Those slimy little baby fingers rubbed against the lenses of my glasses. Spit smears blocked my view. I repeated her mother's name again, but only my mom turned to see little Skylar's palms pressing the glasses firmly into my face.

"Sky," she said in a high-pitched, baby voice.

My mom grabbed Skylar, freeing my arms to stop the little monster from swiping my shades.

Jill finally turned, only to see my mom holding her daughter. She tickled her tummy with her fingers while I stood to the side, ignored, with sun-glasses covered with slobber.

To be clear, my glasses weren't expensive. Smeared spit on the lenses wasn't the end of the world. They weren't from any overrated influencer-endorsed boutique. Don't tell Vince.

There wasn't anything special about them, but I felt special in them. They made me feel a way the family never had, not even once. I wanted to feel like more than just a pair of open ears for these people. Most times, I doubted they even knew my name.

I slipped away from the party into Uncle Rob's apartment, home of the graduate and her family. This was the only bathroom available, four floors down. Of course, the bathroom was occupied.

I sighed. My shoulders slouched forward as I dragged my feet over to the kitchen. I took my sunglasses off and stared out the window toward the lake.

Shaking my head, I ran my sunglasses under the kitchen faucet, cleansing the mirrors of the baby slop and fingerprints. I took my time because I was alone. Every millisecond was a gift, thinking about how long I could get away with hiding in that kitchen.

SEVEN

After the temporary peace, I put my sunglasses on and went back to the rooftop. Climbing the stairs, I saw Uncle Rob coming down. I raised my hand to wave.

All Rob said was, "Look at Mr. Movie Star with his shades over here," while giving me two thumbs up.

My steps slowed as Rob walked past me, laughing.

"Mail me an autograph when you get back to Hollywood, Patrick," he shouted up the stairs.

I always joked around about the family not knowing my name, but that's the day I got proof.

As the celebration rolled on, I found myself in a pretty open area while everyone was either in line for or already eating cake. I was back among the crowd but wasn't socially suffocating. The sun was just a sliver behind the Chicago skyline, turning the sky into a swirling pink and orange mess.

"You're missing out on this scrumptious cake," a voice said as a body passed to my left, disturbing my peaceful moment. "Your mom had to make this."

His name was Dick, yet another uncle of mine. I wasn't sure what gave him that idea. It was clearly a generic, store-bought graduation cake with the plastic cover right next to it on the table. I even saw it from where I stood. The cake wasn't personalized with a name or year, either.

Given his job, he usually had excellent attention to detail. That was putting it nicely. He borderline had obsessive-compulsive disorder.

Dick didn't give me a chance to answer as he parked himself in front of me, his head next to the sun. He started criticizing the cake texture, claiming it "could be a bit less dry" and that the frosting "was a bit heavy" for his liking. Apparently, Dick was a food competition judge when he wasn't a carpenter.

"Do you mind?" he suddenly asked while squinting at me.

I had no clue what he was talking about.

He used his hand, which also held his fork, to move my body ninety degrees to my right. He said the reflection of the sun on my sunglasses was blinding him.

"Ah, that's better," he sighed, before shoveling another forkful of grocery-store cake into his mouth. "I kind of need my eyes working, you know?"

Although Dick married into my family, he kept pace with their social skills, or lack of them. While chewing, he stared into my lenses, once again squinting. He was no longer blinded, but he turned his suntanned, wrinkled face, looking confused.

His hand, still holding that fork, reached forward and grabbed one of the arms of my sunglasses.

My neck and shoulders tensed up. I kept my mouth shut and stood still, wondering what he was up to.

"Your glasses are crooked," he said. He lifted the right side up and down, trying to straighten them on my face. "Here, hold this," Dick said, not asking. He handed me his plate and fork to free up both his hands.

As I stood there holding his half-eaten graduation cake, Dick was hard at work adjusting my sunglasses. Knowing his pickiness, I was surprised he didn't whip out a level from his back pocket. After about ten or so seconds of fiddling, Dick let go and took his cake plate back. He shook his head with sheer disgust.

"I think your nose is crooked, pal," Dick said, as if his son didn't run into me playing kickball in 7th grade, shattering my nose.

His kid had no business running from left field to catch that pop fly in center field. Despite the head-to-head collision, I still made the catch.

EIGHT

Using the shortened line for cake as an excuse,
I left Dick to finish eating. But I had no plans to get
any overpriced, manufactured party cake.

I walked over to an area with some tables. All
of them were pretty full except for one at the end.
One child sat at that table, staring aimlessly at
the other kids running around. I sympathized with
him and his peaceful aloneness. This child looked
about the age of all the other graduates, perhaps
one of Shelby's classmates.

"Is this seat taken?" I politely asked.

"I don't know, is it?" the child answered.

Despite the delivery, that wasn't the rudest

thing someone had said to me that evening.

I sat directly across from him, but the child's eyes didn't really move. He was still and stone-faced. My eyes slid to the chair beside him. I saw a walking stick leaning against it.

This child couldn't see.

"Congratulations on the whole... graduation thing," I said, getting a nod from the kid.

His head moved up slightly after hearing where my voice came from. "Thank you," he said.

I thought the other chairs were empty because his friends were coming back soon, maybe with cake. However, the lack of belongings on the other chairs or the tabletop hinted that he sat utterly alone.

"So, are you looking forward to high school?" I asked.

"Honestly, it's hard to see my future," the child said.

I gritted my teeth with embarrassment. I immediately regretted how I worded my question, since he couldn't technically see anything.

"Because it's so bright," the child added, while a slight smirk pulled at his cheek.

It was infectious. I smiled, too.

He giggled and said he might need to buy a pair of sunglasses. "You know, because of the brightness," he said for emphasis.

I remembered he couldn't see visual cues to show his joke landing. I laughed out loud and took my sunglasses off, sitting them on the generic graduation tablecloth. I stared directly into this kid's eyes.

"I'm Landon," the boy said, still smiling. "What is your name?"

"Michael," I answered.

He asked if I liked the party's music choice.

As we talked, my blue eyes, which my mom took all the credit for, looked down at my mirrored sunglasses. My reflection stared back.

I saw someone who didn't need to stand out to have a normal conversation and didn't need any confidence booster to be social, either. Landon sure didn't.

Without the ability to see, that child, a complete stranger, was nicer than any relative I had met on that rooftop. After looking at their reflections all afternoon, you would think someone in my family could have seen what I saw from behind those lenses.

I suppose that's just a different kind of blind.

About the Author

Born and raised in Chicago, IL, Michael Fergus has spent a decade telling stories through marketing in the business world. Now, he has decided to pursue his passion for storytelling on a personal level. His writing style draws inspiration from both the playful and the painful aspects of life. Loving to get lost in the dramatic and quirky relationships between relatable yet outlandish characters, Michael's ultimate goal is to become a published author in the young adult genre while also writing short stories to hone his skills.

About the Publisher

Storyshares is a publisher focused on supporting the millions of teens and adults who struggle with reading by creating a new shelf in the library specifically for them. The ever-growing collection features content that is compelling and culturally relevant for teens and adults, yet still readable at a range of lower reading levels.

Storyshares generates content by engaging deeply with writers, bringing together a community to create this new kind of book. With more intriguing and approachable stories to choose from, the teens and adults who have fallen behind are improving their skills and beginning to discover the joy of reading.
For more information, visit storyshares.org.

Easy to Read. Hard to Put Down.